ELLIS LOVES POPCORN.
WHO DOESN'T?

But one day her school goes on a healthy eating campaign and her dads decide to follow suit, banning all snack foods from their house, INCLUDING POPCORN. Unfair. Ellis has got to get around that edict, so one night she pops a bag of popcorn out back in the garage… and she's met with more than just her favorite salty snack. One kernel refuses to pop, and soon it's sprouted a face, arms, and legs! He introduces himself as Popcorn Bob, and he is NOT in a good mood. (Ever, really.) He's absolutely ravenous, and no amount of food keeps him from being hangry. Bob causes no end of chaos for Ellis, and she decides to rid herself of him once and for all, except… she actually starts to like him.

A chapter book for all ages, POPCORN BOB is a laugh-out-loud story about the power of friendship, and a perfect bowl of popcorn.

LEVINE QUERIDO

Hey, this is not a final book!

So please don't sell it. And if you're kind enough to write a review, please check any content against the finished book, or with Alexandra Hernandez at alexandra@levinequerido.com.

Some other helpful information...

Pub date: April 20, 2021
ISBN: 978-1-64614-040-4
Price: $14.99
Category: Middle Grade
Age: 7-12
Page Count: 152

For Publicity:

Alexandra Hernandez
alexandra@levinequerido.com

For Foreign Rights: Luciënne van der Leije

l.van.der.leije@singeluitgeverijen.nl

For Domestic Rights:

Linda Biagi
linda@biagirights.com

For Sales:

Levine Querido is distributed by Chronicle Books. To place orders in the U.S., please contact your Chronicle Books sales representative, email order.desk@hbgusa.com, or call customer service toll-free at 800-759-0190.

GETTING OUT THE WORD FOR

POPCORN BOB

3 Reasons We Love This Book

+ A roaring start to an inclusive (gay dads – but that's not what it's about!) new illustrated chapter book series from an award-winning husband and wife duo
+ Illustrations and format recall classic comic strips—making this a great choice for independent reading
+ Popcorn Bob is a zany, cranky (but still loveable) main character who's the cause of sharp, witty humor that kids and parents will laugh with together

Marketing and Publicity Highlights

+ Major early galley distribution (You have one in your hand; our plan worked!)
+ Extensive earned media outreach (Our publicity team is #fiyah!)
+ IG and YouTube advertising (We're coming for you book-tuber-grammers!)
+ Appearances at select festivals and cons (Cosplay all day! amirite?)
+ Virtual events with indie booksellers (Zoom-ing all the way to your heart!)
+ Submit for all major awards (For your consideration…please read our books!)
+ Original #content across LQ's social platforms (Please, like and subscribe!)
+ Outreach to parenting and educator bloggers
+ Activity and coloring sheets are available (Have you heard the popcorn song?)
+ Follow #PopcornBob on Instagram (He's always popping off…)

POPCORN
☆ BOB ☆

POPCORN BOB

MARANKE RINCK

illustrated by **MARTIJN VAN DER LINDEN**

translated by Nancy Forest-Flier

LQ

LEVINE QUERIDO

MONTCLAIR · AMSTERDAM · NEW YORK

This is an Em Querido book
Published by Levine Querido

LQ
LEVINE QUERIDO

www.levinequerido.com · info@levinequerido.com

Levine Querido is distributed by Chronicle Books LLC

Text copyright © 2019 by Maranke Rinck
Illustrations copyright © 2019 by Martijn van der Linden
Translation copyright © 2021 by Nancy Forest-Flier

Originally published in the Netherlands by Querido

Library of Congress Control Number: 2020937501
ISBN 978-1-64614-040-4

Printed and bound in the United States

Published in April 2021
First Printing

Book design by Patrick Collins
The text type was set in Fresco Normal

Martijn van der Linden drew the illustrations for this book with a 2B pencil
on 300 gsm paper while eating a mix of salty and sweet popcorn.

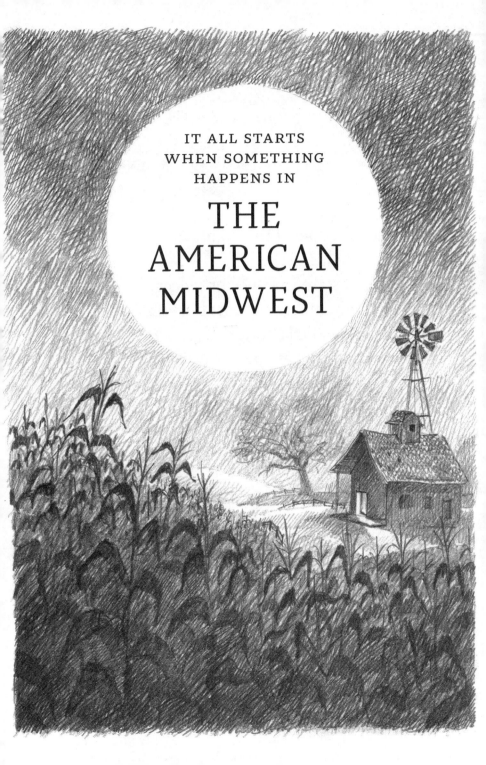

In the middle of the night, Farmer Bill
sneaks outside.
He looks around once or twice.
Then he runs to the cornfield on tiptoe.
He pulls a little bottle
from his pocket and
twists off the cap.

Boy, does it stink!
It smells like rotten eggs.
And burnt plastic.

2

It sinks into the ground, where it fizzes
and sputters.
Bill is pleased.
He holds his nose.
This stuff is super-illegal.
He had to pay a lot of money for it.
No wonder it stinks.
"Grow," Bill whispers to his corn plants.

And so they do.

The next day, the plants
that were fed *Mega-Grow*
are big alright.
Mega big!
At least three feet taller
than all the others!
With mega-big
kernels.

♫ Soon I'll be rich! ♫

But Farmer Bill spoke too soon. His big kernels won't pop, no matter how long he heats them up.

"A pot full of garbage!" he cries angrily. "It's totally useless!"

So he throws the kernels in with the rest of his popcorn.

Then he gives it a good stir and sells the whole mess to the popcorn factory. Just as he always does.

POPCORN & CO

No one will ever know.

THE NETHERLANDS

A LITTLE WHILE LATER

CHAPTER 1

POPCORN MAKES EVERYBODY HAPPY

These are my daddies and me.
The one with the robot shirt is Steve.
The one with the checkered shirt is Gus.
And I'm Ellis.
People who call me Ellis-the-Bellis don't get *any* popcorn.

I make awesome popcorn.
But I don't do anything special.
I just follow the directions
on the box.

POPCORN

Soft as velvet!

Straight from the microwave!

Our popcorn pops every time*.
Each kernel explodes
with a bang.

A treat to eat
and a treat to make!

CRUNCHY

How do you make the tastiest fresh popcorn?

It's easy! Follow the steps on the side of the box.

*Sometimes you get a kernel that won't pop.
Popcorn should never be reheated.

Step 1
Place a bag of popcorn
in the microwave.
Set the correct time.

Step 2
Relax and wait
until all the kernels
have popped.

Step 3
Put the popcorn
in a bowl.

11

Maybe I'm just talented.
Talented at making popcorn, I mean.
There's not much else I can do.

Well, there are handstands.
I can do those, too.
But handstands don't make people happy.

And popcorn makes *everybody* happy.
That's why I pop some every day
after school.

Aren't we forgetting something?

It's almost four o'clock. Come on!

Where are your shoes?

Oh, right, today we have to go to school
for a talk.
I point to the bowl on the table.
It's still full.
"And what about the popcorn?"
"We'll eat it when we get home,"
says Steve.

But I have a better idea.

CHAPTER 2

NICE TO SEE YOU SO CHEERFUL

The four of us are sitting at the
teacher's table.
Ms. Kim is on one side.
We're on the other.
So my fathers look like boys from my class.
Except one has a beard.
And the other one is bald.
That makes me giggle.
"Nice to see you so cheerful,"
says Ms. Kim.

I stop laughing right away.
Then I sneak some popcorn out
of my pocket.
I put it in my mouth before anyone can
see it.
And chew it very slowly.

Ms. Kim takes a piece of paper out of her
desk drawer.
"This drawing is by Ellis."
"Nice!" says Steve.
He gives it a thumbs-up.

Gus winks at me.
If they really were boys from my class,
they'd be my friends.
I'm sure of it.
I push some popcorn into Gus's hand.
And I wink back.

"Look," says Ms. Kim.
"The children were supposed to draw
self-portraits.

On one side is their normal head.
On the other side is what's *inside*
their head.
You know what I mean."

Just to be clear:
we were *not* supposed to draw our *brains*.
That's what Dante did, the boy who lives
next door to us.
He had to start all over again,
even though they were super
good brains.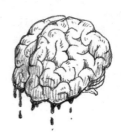
With veins and everything.
I almost forgot that he always
calls me Ellis-the-Bellis.

"The children had to draw their dreams;
what they think about," Ms. Kim explains.
"A pet or a soccer trophy, that kind
of thing.
But Ellis drew ...
Well, you can see for yourself."

I'm glad she showed off my drawing.
Dante can draw much better than I can,
but mine still looks pretty
good. It makes me feel
like giving
everybody
a treat.

I empty my coat pockets and scatter the
popcorn on the table.
Ms. Kim looks as if I'd scattered my *brains*
on the table.
Doesn't she like popcorn?
Gus tries to scoop all of it onto his lap,
as fast as he can.
But most of it falls on the floor.
The popcorn rolls through
the classroom.
My fathers drop to their knees.
They use their hands to sweep it up.
You can see a little of Gus's
white bottom.
I can tell that Ms. Kim sees it, too.
Just then her phone starts beeping.

"Well. Our time is up."
Ms. Kim stands up.
Pieces of popcorn crunch under her shoes.
My fathers scramble to their feet.
"There's something else I have to tell you,"
she says.
"We're going to make The Rainbow a
healthy school.
A school without candy, cookies, or soda.
And that means no popcorn.
Everyone will get an e-mail telling them
all about it.
But I wanted you to know right away.
You understand why."
Ms. Kim walks to the door and opens it.
"So nice to meet with you again."
My fathers nod.
Then they pull me out of the classroom,
into the hall.

CHAPTER 3

THE POPCORN PARADISE

Weird that Ms. Kim doesn't like popcorn. She could see your butt, by the way.

Gus pulls up his pants.
"You know, that teacher of yours…"
he says.
"She has a point.
How about shifting gears?"
"What are gears?" I ask.
"And how do you shift them?"

Steve nods, like he thinks this is the best
idea *ever*.
"Then all you have to do is start making
salads," he says to me.
"Instead of popcorn.
I'm sure you're good at that, too."
I can feel myself getting a tiny bit worried.

When we get home, they take the
microwave out of the cabinet.

We won't be needing this anymore.

Now I'm getting really worried.
"You're not going to throw it away,
are you?" I ask.
Gus takes a picture with his phone.
"No. I'm going to sell it.
And until it's sold, it stays in the shed."
Now I'm super worried.

I don't eat much that night.
"I don't feel so good," I mutter.
"You'll get used to it, Ellis," says Steve.
He shoves a spoonful of beets
into his mouth.
When they're finally finished, I tell them
I'm going to my room.
But I don't really do that, of course.

Our shed is dark and small.
And it's crammed full of old stuff.
But as soon as I flip the light switch,
it feels like I've gone to heaven.
Ta-daaa!
There's the microwave, gleaming
in the light.
Next to it is a stack of popcorn boxes.
I quickly shut the door of the shed and
stick the plug into a nearby socket.
And sure enough, IT WORKS!
I jump up and down.
This is great!
The shed will be my secret
popcorn paradise.

CHAPTER 4

THE BIGGEST POPCORN KERNEL EVER

What's this?

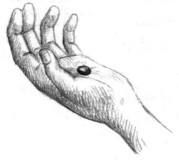

That's weird.
My kernels always pop, every single one of them.
On the box it says you should never put a kernel in the microwave twice.
But I'm in charge here.
So I just stick the kernel back in.

The microwave hums for a minute or two.
The kernel grows, but it doesn't pop.
It gets bigger and bigger.
I didn't know that corn could grow
like that.
Now the kernel is as big as a shiny
yellow lemon.
Any minute now it's going to explode,
I'm sure of it.

But something else happens.

Two little legs pop out of the kernel!
And two little arms.
And…what?
That's impossible…

The kernel has turned into a little man!
I stare at him.
And he looks back at me, furious.

The little corn man
waves his little fists.
He takes a couple
of steps and falls
on his back.

He thrashes his little
arms and legs in the air,
just like a beetle.

In the meantime,
the plate he's lying on
keeps turning around
and around.
The little man struggles
to pull himself up.

He crawls to the door
and pounds on it.

I wait a few seconds, but finally I open
the door.
The microwave stops right away. It smells
like fire.

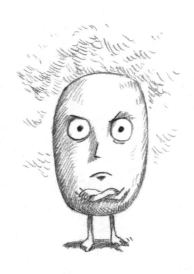

Now that the kernel isn't behind glass
he looks *much* bigger.
And *much* angrier.
He waves in some fresh air and looks
at me with fierce little eyes.
Then he crosses his arms.

"Sooo," he says.
"What were you thinking, little girl?
I'll let him spin around a bit longer?
I'm sure he'll love it?"

Well?
Is that what you
were thinking?

CHAPTER 5

LET ME INTRODUCE MYSELF

"Let me introduce myself,"
says the little man.
"I'm Bob.
Popcorn Bob.
And I'm really hungry."

Suddenly I understand what's going on.
"You're not real," I say.
"Oh, no?" Bob asks.
"Of course not," I say.

I'm glad it didn't take me long to figure
this out.
So this is what an imaginary friend
looks like.

"What are you looking at?"
asks the little man.
I squeeze my eyes shut and shake
my head.
Maybe then things will go back to normal,
and I'll stop seeing little men.
But when I open my eyes,
Bob is still there.
He taps his forehead with his finger.

I sit down and shut my eyes again.
I'm waiting for the little guy to disappear.
But soon I feel something tickling me.
As if a mouse were running up my leg
to my shoulder.
It gives me goose bumps.

It's Bob.
Didn't you hear me?
I'm hungry!

I take the little
man off my
shoulder.
"Bob," I say.
"Listen."
He turns
away from me.
"I'm listening."

"I love popcorn," I say.

Bob nods.

"Of course you do. Do you have some for me?"

What's he talking about?

He *is* popcorn.

So he doesn't *eat* popcorn, does he?

"Shh," I say.

"What I wanted to say is this: I love *normal* popcorn.

Popcorn that doesn't talk.

That doesn't get hungry. Get it?"

"Wow," Bob mutters. "No manners."

"I don't need an imaginary friend," I say, louder.

"I bet Louie would love you! He's the little boy next door.

But I just turned nine last week.

I'm much too old for imaginary friends!"

Bob trembles in my hand.

As if there were a battery inside him.

He looks angrier than ever.

Then suddenly...

Bob explodes!
He turns into a super
big piece of white
popcorn.
He jumps up, flies
through the shed,
and roars.
Loud.

Bob bounces
from the
lamp to
the window.
And then
he falls to
the floor.

Where he carries
on like a crazy
windup toy.

Finally he's turned into popcorn!
A super big piece of popcorn at that.
But one with eyes and arms and everything.
Even so, he *is* just popcorn.
And I *love* popcorn.
One big bite and that would be the end of
this whole weird mess.
I pick him up and open my mouth wide.
The piece of popcorn stares back at me.
He's really angry.
He waves his fists.

Suddenly he bites my finger.
"Hey, you!" I shout.
"I can't eat you, but you can eat me?"

Then I hear something outside.
Footsteps, on the gravel.

CHAPTER 6

REAL
OR NOT REAL?

The footsteps come closer.
I shove Popcorn Bob into the pocket
of my sweater.
He just fits.
I pretend I'm asleep.
The door of the shed opens.
"Ellis?" Steve asks.
"Are you in here?"
I sit up and stretch, yawning.
Daddy sticks his nose
in the air.
He sniffs.
"Unbelievable,"
he says.

I'm caught.
He knows I've made popcorn.
This is the end of my paradise.
I peek at the microwave.
You can see the edge of the empty
bag inside.
But Steve doesn't suspect a thing.

I stare at him in amazement.
Does he really not know what I've done?

"That's why I'm sitting here," I blurt out.
"I'm not allowed to eat popcorn.
But at least here I can still smell it."
I look at him with sad, puppy dog eyes.

Oh, Ellis.
Were you screaming in here because
you can't have any popcorn?

Was I screaming?

Daddy nods.
"We could even hear it in the house."

I feel a cold shiver.
It was Bob who screamed.
Not me.
But Daddy heard it, too.
So I'm *not* making this up.
Is Bob real?
I find out soon enough.
Because he pinches me in the side.

And that *really* hurts.
"Owww," I groan softly.

Daddy doesn't notice.
"You want to come in with me?" he asks.
"We have a nice healthy dessert."
"I'll be right in," I tell him.

As soon as he's gone, I take Bob out
of my pocket.
He's changed back into a yellow kernel
of corn.
He says:

Give me
something to eat
right now.

"Okay, okay," I tell him.
"But don't let my fathers know about you.
Otherwise they'll find out that I was
secretly making popcorn.
So sit still and DON'T pinch!"
I put him back in my pocket.
And walk through the yard to the house.

CHAPTER 7

FANTASTIC CAKE

Steve puts a couple of little forks
on the table.
Gus gives me a worried look.

I shrug.
I have a live piece of popcorn in my pocket.

A hungry one, with arms and legs.
And when he gets angry, he explodes.
"I'm okay," I say.
"Sort of."

They've made a kind of cake.
"With chocolate, but without sugar,"
Steve says proudly.

He cuts three slices.
"And with cauliflower.
But according to the
recipe you can't taste it."
"I still don't feel so good," I lie.
"Just cut me a thin slice."
I feel Bob moving in my pocket.
"You can have it all," I say under
my breath.
No way am I going to eat cake with
cauliflower.

I let a chunk of cake slide into my pocket.
My fathers didn't see a thing.
They're talking about rubber duckies.
That's what they do for a living.

Steve designs them.

I stick more cake in my pocket.
I'm beginning to like this.
But suddenly both my fathers look at me.

I take a quick bite of cake.
Oh, dear.
It tastes like cold cauliflower.
"Mmm," I say, and give them
a thumbs-up.
Steve laughs.
"For a minute there I thought you were
putting the cake in your pocket."
"Of course not," I say.

I'm going to eat every bite.

Then I feel something on my back.
It really tickles.
It's Bob!

I try to push him farther down.
"What is it?" my fathers ask.
"Oh, nothing," I say.
I bend my arm in a strange position.
"A little itch."
I try to grab Bob.
But he keeps
crawling away.
Now he's on my
neck, under my hair.
What's he doing,
anyway?

BURP!

At just that moment
Bob burps.
BURP!
"Eww!" I shout, and
jump to my feet.
My fathers look
at me as if I came
from Mars.

"You okay?" Steve asks.
I push Bob back down.
They're sure to see him!
"My tummy feels weird," I say.
"I think I'll go to bed.
But I'll take another piece of this delicious
cake with me.
In case I get hungry later on.
You don't have to check up on me."
I blow them a few kisses.
And run
out of the
living room.

Night-night!
Sleep tight!

CHAPTER 8

SO WHAT? YOU'RE ALIVE, TOO!

Upstairs, I put the horrible cake on my desk.

And I pull Bob out of my hair.

He looks at me with gleaming little eyes.

"Don't look so happy," I say.

"My fathers think I'm going crazy.

You know you were supposed to stay in my pocket, right?"

"But I was so hungry," says Bob.

"Have you got any more of that fantastic cake?"

He jumps onto my desk.

He eats it all and licks the plate clean.
Then he climbs onto my bed.

I just stand there watching him.
"Who are you, really?" I ask.
"There must be something wrong with
your ears," Bob says.
"I'm Bob.
Popcorn Bob. I already told you."
"Yeah, yeah," I say.
"But you're alive!"

"So what? You're alive, too!"
"But I'm a human being," I say.

I don't have time to think about Bob.
I've got something else to take care of.
The microwave.
I *can't* let them sell it.
Otherwise I'll only be eating healthy
things for the rest of my life.

I got Gus's old laptop for my birthday.
I open it up.
Then I plop down on the bed next to Bob.
I find my fathers' listing.
And I make a really high bid
on the microwave.
Under a fake name, of course.
There we go.
Five hundred euros, from Mrs. Silly van
Silly in Crazydam.
No one will ever bid more than that.
They'll never sell that microwave.

After a little searching I find another
website.
It's the site of a factory, Popcorn & Co.
We always buy their popcorn.
But I can't find anything about
live kernels.
I bite my nails.
How am I supposed to know what to do
with Bob?
I'm only nine!

The factory must know more than what
they put on their website.
So I'll send them an e-mail.

From: Ellis
Sent: Tuesday, July 2, 2019, 8:13 p.m.
To: popcorn&co@gmail.com
Subject: popcorn

Dear factory,

I always make your popcorn.
But today one of the kernels came to life.
His name is Bob.
He gets angry very easily.
And he's always hungry.
You can see that this might be a big problem.
Does it happen often?
And what should I do about it?

Bye-bye,
Ellis

In the middle of the
night I hear a sound
that wakes me up.
Dripping?
Maybe not.
Little feet running across the floor.
My eyes fly open.
It's dark, but a strip of light falls
into the room.
The door is open a crack.
"Bob?" I whisper.
There's no answer.

Bob is not in my room.
He's not in the hallway, either.
It's strangely quiet in the house, because
my fathers have already gone to bed.

I look in the bathroom.

Bob is nowhere to be seen.
I go downstairs.
He's not in the living room.
He's not in the downstairs bathroom.
Not even in the kitchen.

Then I hear a scream.

CHAPTER 9

I'M NO MOUSE

That was Gus!

I run back upstairs.

Steve is stretched out on his back.

He's asleep.

But Gus is curled up, clutching his pillow.

He points to the end of the bed with a trembling finger.

Standing next to Steve's big toe is Bob.

"A mouse," Gus whispers.

I snatch Bob from the bed and hide him
in my hands.
Luckily Gus isn't wearing his glasses.
"Be careful or he'll bite!" he says.

Bob tries to wriggle loose.
He really will bite if I don't watch out!
"It's just a little mouse," I say.
"Go back to sleep, Dad."

I'll put
him outside.

Gus lies back down.
He's very grateful.
"Daughters are so brave,"
I hear him say.
I quickly pull the
bedroom door closed.

I throw Bob on my bed.
"A mouse," he says.
He almost spits the word out.
"Do you think I have a tail?"
I shake my head.
Bob starts quivering.
"Do I have those strange little ears?"
Now he's quivering all over.
"Or whiskers?
Listen, I'm talking to you.
DO I HAVE WHISKERS?"
I shake my head.

No!
Don't MESS with me!
I'm no MOUSE!
AAAAH!

Bob explodes.
I throw my blanket over him,
and just in time.
It looks like there's a fight going on under
the blanket.
"My father couldn't see you very well
without his glasses," I say.
"And a good thing, too.
Otherwise you would have been
discovered!
What were you doing there anyway?"
Bob calms down at once.
The blanket stops moving.
Then his head appears.

In the kitchen, Bob eats two peanut butter
sandwiches.
Three apples.
Four bananas.
And fourteen candy cola gummies.
(I didn't even know we had them!)
I stare at him.
"You're just like the Very Hungry
Caterpillar," I say.
Bob gives me an angry look.

CHAPTER 10

NO OTHER CHOICE

For the rest of the night I can't sleep
a wink.
Bob can't sleep either.
He's "letting his food digest."
But now it's Friday morning.
And I have to go to school.
Bob can't stay home alone.
My fathers work in the attic.
That's where their office is.

Soon I'm outside,
with Bob in my coat pocket.
I have no idea how I'm going to keep
him secret.

Hey, if it isn't Ellis-the-Bellis!

That's Dante and his little brother Louie.
"Keep still, Bob," I whisper.

You got any popcorn?

I feel Bob moving
in my pocket.
And I shake my head.
"My fathers won't let me eat
popcorn anymore."
"Too bad," says Dante.
I shrug my shoulders.
"You wouldn't get any anyway.
My name isn't Ellis-the-Bellis!"
Dante laughs.
I stick out my tongue.

And me?

I pat Louie's hood.
"You would for sure.
Because you're
a tiger."

Dante takes Louie to the kindergarten classroom.
I hang up my coat and take Bob out.
"I'm going to put you in the pocket of my sweater now," I whisper.

Don't make any noise in the classroom. Be as quiet as a mouse.

Bob grumbles.

67

"I have something important to tell you,"
says Ms. Kim.
"But first I want you all to be
perfectly quiet."
She presses her finger to her lips.

Slowly the buzzing of voices stops.
But I can still hear *one little voice*.
And it isn't far away.

"Hungry," I hear.
The whole class turns to me.
I put my hand in my pocket.
I want to give Bob a pinch.
I want to warn him to keep his
mouth shut.
But I don't dare.
He might bite my finger again.
Instead I stroke his belly.
At least I hope it's his belly.
I used to have a hamster named Sally.
She always fell asleep when I stroked her.
I hope it works.

CHAPTER 11

HEALTHIER THAN CHOCOLATE

Bob starts wiggling all around my pocket.
"Hee hee hee," I hear him giggle.
"Ha ha ha!"
Oh, no.
I stop stroking him right away.
But the giggling in my pocket doesn't stop.
"Shhh," I whisper.
"Don't laugh."
Fay points to me.

Ms. Kim presses her finger harder against her lips.
Luckily even Bob quiets down.
"Our school is going to be a *healthy* school," she tells us.
I roll my eyes.
I've heard this before.
"We're all going to get nice and fit," she says.
"Your parents will be sent an e-mail explaining everything.
We start after the weekend.
So: don't bring any more cookies or candy to school.
Only healthy things."
Then she looks straight at me.

And that means no popcorn.

Josh raises his hand.
"Not even for birthdays?"
"No."
"Not even during recess?" asks Anne.
"Bring some nice fruit or vegetables,"
says Ms. Kim.

But popcorn is corn

That's really healthy!

Ms. Kim frowns.
"Popcorn is a big fat mouthful
of air.
With salt or sugar.
And it makes a mess in the classroom."
I can feel Bob getting all worked up.
I look at the floor.
There are still a few pieces of popcorn left
from yesterday.
Ms. Kim kicks them aside with her shoe.
"It's true, Ellis. Popcorn is just plain junk!"

Bob explodes in my pocket.
"WHAAAT?" he roars.
All I can do is roar with him.
"WHAAAT!" I scream.
And I jump to my feet.
My chair tips over.
"WHAAAT... I mean is, I have to go
to the bathroom!"
I race out of the classroom.

Be right back!

CHAPTER 12

WHO IS THAT PERSON?

I lock the door of the bathroom.
Bob crawls out of my pocket.
He's changed again into a big white piece
of popcorn.
"What am I going to do
with you?" I mutter.
Bob is trembling with rage.

Who is
that person?

"That's Ms. Kim," I say.
Bob jumps up and down.

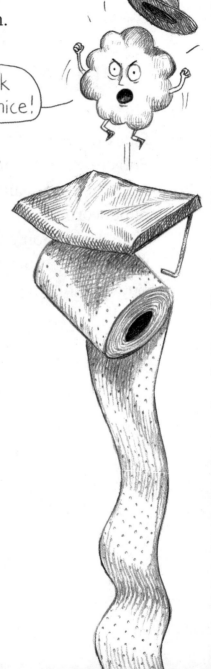

I don't think
she's very nice!

"I don't think so either,"
I say.
"But you have to calm
down, Bob!
You'll give us away if
you make
so much noise."
"Popcorn isn't junk,"
he says.
"Of course not," I say.
"Popcorn is fantastic."
Bob is suddenly quiet.
He looks at me.
"Do you really
think so?"

76

"Here's the thing," I say.
"We can't let her find out about you.
Otherwise she'll know that I've made
popcorn, and I'm not supposed to.
Then my fathers will really get rid of
the microwave.
We can't let that happen!
I need popcorn, every day.
It makes me happy."
Bob nods.
Does he really understand me?
Now he's turned into a big yellow
kernel again.
I put him back in my pocket.
Along with a piece of gingerbread.
He's quiet for the rest of the morning.

But during recess Bob starts acting
up again.
He steals a piece of cake from Burak's
backpack.

During spelling he keeps calling out the wrong answers.

And who gets blamed for it?

CHAPTER 13

I'M A GOOD READER

Ms. Kim thinks I need to practice reading.
On my own, in the hall.
But I'm a good reader.
Just not if I have to read *fast*.
And Ms. Kim likes fast.
I have three minutes to rattle off as many
words as I can.
I look at the paper.
"Doughnut," I read.
"Waitress."
"Hamburger."

Moonlight.
Candle light.
napkin.

V...eg...vegetable.

What a pain in the neck.
I take Bob out of my pocket.
Maybe he can cheer me up.
But he looks at me in astonishment.

What was that all about?

"Moonlight, candlelight...
That's a terrible story!"

"I'm practicing for a test," I explain.
"Makes me hungry," says Bob.
I sigh.
"My food is all gone.
And no more stealing."
"Not even an apple?"
"No."
"A grape?"
"No."
"How about a teeny tiny little grape?"
Bob is starting to shake.

School
is stupid!

Oh, no. Here comes Mr. Mike.
He's the principal.
And he's pretty nice.
He always wears crazy
colored sneakers.
Today they're green.
As green as grass in the sunshine.
He's almost skipping down the hall.
But this is not a good time for skipping.
Bob is freaking out.
He explodes.
And he changes back
into a big white piece
of popcorn.
He goes flying way
up in the air.
And hits Mr. Mike
right in the face.

"You doofus!" I shout.
Then I freeze. Uh-oh.
Naturally Mr. Mike thinks I mean *him*.
He presses his hand to his eye.

What was that?

A wad of paper?

I nod slowly.

Uh... sorry,
Mr. Mike.

CHAPTER 14

AND WHAT
ABOUT BOB?

I'm waiting in the hall.
Bob is back in my pocket.
Mr. Mike is in my classroom
talking with Ms. Kim.
I hope I don't get detention,
or worse.

Come with me. I'm teaching the eighth grade today. You can work in my office.

Not bad!
At least I don't have to worry
about Bob in here.
He's grumbling at the top of his
lungs, but no one can hear him.
I'm doing my arithmetic.
And sometimes I even forget he's there.

But when I look up, I can't believe my eyes.
My pocket is empty.
Bob is sitting on Mr. Mike's desk biting
into a Mars Bar.

"So, Ellis," I hear someone say.
Mr. Mike walks into the office with a stack
of binders.
He puts them on his desk.
Bob runs off just in time.
Mr. Mike gives me a friendly look.
"You don't have to be worried, you know.
I just heard from Ms. Kim that Houba has
brought in some treats for everyone."
And it's true.

Houba just got a baby sister.
"You worked hard in here," says Mr. Mike.

So you can go back to your class.

But what about Bob?
Where is he?
I look all around.
Then, very slowly, I gather up my things.
"Hurry up, Ellis," says Mr. Mike.

Or all the treats will be gone.

I walk slowly to the door, dragging
my feet.
My eyes run over every inch of the office.
I can't see Bob anywhere.
"Shut the door behind you," says Mr. Mike
without looking up.
And just as I'm about to do that, Bob runs
past me.
He slips into the hall.
But he doesn't wait for me there.

He runs straight into my classroom.
On the cabinet near the coat rack are
Houba's treats, a big plate of sugar cookies
with pink candy sprinkles on top.
Everybody brings these treats to school
when they get a baby sister or brother.
But is it okay with Ms. Kim?
I don't have time to think about this
problem, because Bob is already
on the cabinet.
And he's started to munch his way
through the treats like crazy.

chomp
chomp
chomp

The rest of the day is a disaster.
The whole class thinks I've eaten
the treats.
Houba won't look at me anymore.
Dante won't even say Ellis-the-Bellis to me.
And then Mr. Mike comes into
the classroom.
He walks right up to me.
"Tell me honestly, Ellis," he says.
He waves an empty candy wrapper
in the air.

Did you eat my Mars Bar?

I shake my head no.

Mr. Mike looks around the classroom.

"Then who stole my Mars Bar?"

He even looks at Ms. Kim, who turns
as white as a sheet.

"And what were you doing with a Mars
Bar?" she asks.

Mr. Mike stares at her.

"Uh…I…uh…

for…emergencies?"

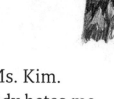

Why don't we just forget about
being a healthy school?

"That's enough, Ellis," says Ms. Kim.

I have detention, and everybody hates me.

CHAPTER 15

STOP ALL THAT BOUNCING AROUND!

I run.
I run all the way home from school.
With big steps.
As if I were walking on the moon.

"STOP ALL THAT BOUNCING AROUND!"
Bob shouts from my pocket.
But I don't care.
All I can think about is one thing:
popcorn.
A bowl of fresh, crisp popcorn.
And all of it for me.

Ring.
Ring.
Ring!!!

I open our mail slot.

"Ha ha! You're kissing the door!"
I turn around.
The boy from next door is laughing his
head off.
"I don't think my fathers are home,"
I tell him.

Maybe they've been eaten. By a tiger.

Before I can say a word,
the front door opens.

"Hey, there you are," says Steve.
He's wearing a suit.
"Come in quick."
I throw down my backpack.
"Not so noisy.
A couple of our customers are here.
How about coming upstairs with me.
Then you can say hello."

But then go to your room and play nicely, okay?

Sometimes they think I'm still four,
just like Louie.
"Sure," I say.
This is the perfect chance to sneak out
to the shed.

Standing in the upstairs office are a man
and a woman.
My fathers are acting very nervous.
There are at least a hundred rubber
duckies lying on the floor.
In all shapes and sizes.

Of course *this* is when Bob decides to get
out of my pocket.
He crawls across my back, which he likes
to do.
It really tickles.
I burst out laughing when I shake the
woman's hand.
She gives me a friendly nod.

Now it's tickling so much that I don't
think I can stop laughing.
"This is Ellis," says Gus, trying hard
to be calm.
"Go on and play now, honey.
We're going to be busy here for a while."
But the man sticks out *his* hand, too.
I tiptoe between the rubber duckies
to shake it.
And accidentally step on one of them.

SQUEAK!

The squeak startles me, and I stumble.
One second later I'm lying in a sea of
rubber duckies.

I try to straighten out as many as I can,
but it's not easy.
"I'm sorry!"
I can't even look at my fathers.
And then I feel it.
Bob isn't on my neck anymore.

I spot him right away.
He isn't moving a muscle.

No one seems to notice him.
Even so, I don't waste any time.
I dive right on top of him.
"Ellis!" my fathers both shout.
"Sorry, sorry, sorry!"
This time I don't try to straighten the
duckies out.
With Bob hidden in my hands I run out
of the room.

CHAPTER 16

MEH

Soon I'm back in the shed.
I'm making popcorn.
And luckily every kernel pops.
I already feel a lot better, here in my
popcorn paradise.
Bob is eating with me.
But he doesn't look very happy.
"Are you feeling all right?" I ask.
"Meh," he says.

"Maybe you shouldn't eat popcorn," I say.
"After all, people don't eat people."

I give him a worried look.
Bob's yellow color is fading.
His skin used to be shiny, but now it's
starting to wrinkle.

"I want to go back in," he says.
He points to the microwave.
But I'm not sure.
"PUT ME BACK IN!" he shouts.
Then he falls down.
His eyes are shut.
I pick him up quickly and do what he says.

Once he's in the microwave, Bob changes.
It only takes a minute.
But soon he's a shiny popcorn kernel
again.
As big as a lemon.

I breathe a sigh of relief.
But then I'm confused.
Bob is a first-class nuisance.
Because of him, everyone is mad at me.
So why am I glad that he feels better?
"How often do you have to go back in
that thing?" I ask.
"I dunno," says Bob.
"Only when I need to."

That night my fathers are walking on air.
The customers were really impressed
by their work.

They'll let us know soon if we can make new rubber duckies for them.

And we've also had a terrific offer for the microwave!

Unfortunately we're still eating
health food.
Fish with green snot.
Gus calls it whitefish on a bed of bok choy.
I smuggle most of it into my room.
And as Bob slurps it down, I look
at my laptop.
I have an e-mail.
From America!

The e-mail is in English.
So I get the internet to translate it into
Dutch for me.

Hello, dear Ms. Ellis,

Our sincere apologies.
We regret that you had a problem
with our popcorn.
The answer is no; that is in no way
the intention.
Our popcorn is not supposed to change into
a living creature.
Kindly accept a new box of good,
delicious popcorn.
And we ask you please put your bad kernel
in a box, pack it up, and send it
to this address:

Popcorn & Co.
Strange Things
P.O. Box 126724
Francesville, Indiana 47946
United States of America

I look at Bob.
He's relaxing again and digesting
his meal.
It's the only time he's ever peaceful.
I can't just stick him in a box, can I?
But what am I supposed to do?

CHAPTER 17

ENOUGH
IS ENOUGH

It's Saturday morning, much too early.
Another night without sleep.
I had to go downstairs three times to get
more food for Bob.
I had to pull him away from my
fathers' door.
And I had to search for him among
the rubber duckies in the attic.
So I've made a decision.
Enough is enough.
Bob has to go.

We're going for a ride.

Out in the countryside, just the two of us.

Have you got enough food?

Yes, I have enough food.
I'm even taking the microwave.
It's strapped to the back of my bike.
After all, I don't want Bob to turn into a
dried-out raisin.

I bike really fast.
We zoom out of the city.

Before long I'm out in the woods.
The ground here is sandy.
The trees are a hundred shades of green.
It smells like earth and grass.
You can do handstands everywhere.
I think Bob will like it here.
It's much nicer than in the city.
But he's making weird little sounds.
Wait a minute; he's singing.

De do do do,
de da da da!

I told you so! The woods make him happy.
It's better this way.
"Really," I say out loud.
I'm going to find someone who can take
care of Bob.
That will solve everything.
Maybe I can even come visit him.

Suddenly we can't go any farther.
The path is full of sheep.
"Wow!" shouts Bob.
He thinks the sheep are beautiful.
He jumps off the bike.
"Not too close!" I call out.

"They'll trample you!"
But of course Bob doesn't listen.

I look all around.
Does this flock have a shepherd?
Or are they walking around on their own?

A shepherd would be good for Bob, I think.
Someone who's in charge of a flock
of sheep.
He'd easily be able to handle a popcorn
kernel with temper tantrums.
"Baaah!" Bob suddenly bleats.
It sounds just like the real thing.

But the sheep don't
think it's so great.

Baaah!

They start running
all over the place,
bleating loudly.
Bob must have insulted them.
"Come back here!" I call to him.

Suddenly a black-and-white spot
shoots past.
What was that?

CHAPTER 18

SOUP CHICKENS!

The black-and-white spot is a dog.
He races around the sheep in circles.
Running low to the ground.
He's like a magician.
In a few seconds all the sheep are calmed
down and packed close together.
But then Bob decides to do the same thing.

He runs around the flock, too, whooping
and waving his arms.
But that doesn't calm the sheep down.
No, they start stampeding!

I lay my bike down and run after Bob.
It's a miracle I can catch him so quickly.

I get back on my bike.
A little farther on I stop at a farm.
It's at the edge of a field.
It seems to me that ... Yes! Corn plants!
This *must* be a sign.

I take the microwave off my bike.
Then I lug it to the front door.
My mind is made up.
I straighten my coat and knock.
I really hope this will be Bob's new home.
Suddenly I hear screaming.
And then, angry cackling.
"Bob!" I shout.

First I have to push aside twelve hungry
chickens.
And one rooster.
Only then can I rescue Bob.
He's trembling.
He's so angry that he bursts out
of his skin.
But I think he's a little scared, too.

It takes ten minutes for Bob to calm down.
We're sitting in a little field next
to the farm.
I sigh.
"So you can't live here either."
Oops. Did I say that out loud?
Bob stares at me.
"Live?
What do you mean?"

I live with you, don't I?

I'm a little ashamed of myself.
I jump to my feet.
"Well," I say.
"Nobody's home here anyway.
We'll talk about it later.
I'll go get the microwave."
But when I get back, Bob is gone.

I look all over the farmyard.
In the hay barn.
Inside a tractor.
Then I see those rotten chickens again.
But they're calmly pecking at the ground.
Bob isn't there.
He's not in the cornfield either.
Or the vegetable garden.
And not in the empty doghouse.

Bob is really gone.

My cheeks are burning.
There's a knot in my stomach.
My heart is pounding.

"Bob!" I call out.
"Bob, come back!
Come and have something to eat!"
No answer.
The world starts to get blurry.
I wipe my eyes with my sleeve.
"I brought some nice healthy muffins,"
I murmur.

CHAPTER 19

GONE

I strap the microwave to my bike.
And slowly ride away.
I don't pay any attention to where
I'm going.
I'm just searching for Bob.
I look at every blade of grass.
Every leaf on the ground.
"Bonehead," I say to myself.
Bob is gone.
He's gone!

And I think it's awful.

I pedal faster.
"Numbskull!" I scream.
I race ahead.
The wind is blowing through my hair.

Just then I hear the sound
of grouchy groaning.

My heart skips a beat.
I squeeze my brakes hard.

Bob is lying on the side of the road.
His eyes are closed.
His tummy is heaving up and down.
I pick him up and bring him close
to my face.
And before I know it...I give him a kiss.

His eyes fly open.

Bob rubs his face like crazy.
Then he scrambles to his feet in my hand.
He points to my nose.
"Ellis, you are NOT my prince.
I am NOT your princess.
There will be NO kissing around here!"

I grin.
Bob is back.
And he's alive!
I giggle at his angry face.
"That sure is a hyena laugh!" says Bob.
But his eyes are twinkling.
"I'm hungry!"

After that I can't stop.
I laugh so hard my stomach hurts.
I laugh and laugh, on and on.
But the knot in my stomach is gone.
Bob is back.
And I'm never going to let him go.

Bob eats a muffin.
But it doesn't really help.
He's weak, and he's getting paler
by the second.
"I want to go in," he says.
He points to the microwave.
But of course it doesn't work without
electricity.
What am I going to do?
I bike through the woods like crazy.
Until we get to a birdwatcher's hut.
"Please let there be a socket in there,"
I mutter.

Soon Bob is back to his old self.
We eat sandwiches on the dock.
I'm so happy I do a handstand.
Bob looks at me with wide eyes.
"That's brilliant," he whispers.
"How do you DO that?"
I show him how.
And for the rest of the afternoon Bob
practices standing on his head.

We bike back home.
The sun is shining on my face.
I pedal nice and slow.
"You wanted to dump me," Bob says
suddenly.
I gulp.
"I'm sorry, Bob.
Sorry, sorry, sorry.
I, uh…It was a mistake.
But you kept running away!
You know, sometimes you're a little…"

For the first time Bob and I have a good
long talk.
I don't know what made him turn into
a living kernel.

I don't know either,
but I wish I did.

So I promise that
together we'll
find out.
And *he* promises
to do his best
to stay hidden.

CHAPTER 20

BOB THE RUBBER DUCKY

We're back home.
There's a red-and-yellow delivery van
parked out front.

A young man in a cap is just about to ring
the doorbell.
"Hello!" I call out.
I get off my bike.
The delivery man turns around.
"Special delivery from America for Ms....
Ellis?"

"That's me."
He hands me the box.
It's big, but it's not very heavy.
There are all kinds of stamps and
stickers on it.

Louie comes up on his scooter.
He looks curious.
"What's in there?" he asks.
"And why do you have an oven
on your bike?"
"In case I get hungry while I'm biking,"
I tell him.

I go around back and into the shed.
There I open the box.

"Food!" Bob shouts happily.
I grin.
I've never seen so many boxes
of popcorn before.
It gives me an idea.
"You know what I'm going to do?" I ask.

"Eat!" Bob shouts again.
I nod.
"But I'm also going to share it.
On Monday, at school.
Secretly, of course.
With Dante and Louie.
And with Houba and the other kids
in my class."
"So they'll like you again?" Bob asks.
I nod.
"You think it'll work?" I ask.

Bob promises to stay in the shed until
I come back.
I just want to see how angry my
fathers are.
I've never been away so long without
asking permission.
But I didn't have to worry.
"There's our dear daughter!" shouts Gus.
Steve ruffles my hair.
"Have you been on an adventure?"
I nod, very surprised.
"Great!" he says.
"We have super good news."
I frown.

Did you sell the microwave?

My fathers laugh.
"That offer was such a fake.
Who would pay five hundred euros for
that old thing?"
I laugh nervously.
"No, it's something else," they continue.
"You remember that new customer
yesterday?"
I can see myself lying on the floor.
In a sea of rubber duckies.
Steve is beaming.
"They want me to design for them.
They loved the rubber duckies, they said,
especially the one with the cowboy hat.
But Ellis..."
My fathers are hiccupping with laughter.

We don't even have a cowboy rubber ducky!

I nod slowly.
I think I'm beginning to understand.
"So I made a quick sketch," says Steve.
"Look, this is him.
We just have to come up with a name."

"Bob," I blurt out.
My fathers clap their hands.
"Perfect!
Bob the Rubber Ducky."

My fathers want to celebrate their success.
Steve opens all the kitchen cabinets.

I've sort of had it with all that healthy stuff. How about you guys?

Gus looks mischievous.
"Good thing we didn't sell the microwave.
What do you think, Ellis?
How about a good old-fashioned
popcorn party?"

For a minute I don't say a thing.
Then I shake my head.
"No ...
I'd rather eat healthy food."

THE END*

* Well, in America something else is happening.
Something important…

MEANWHILE, BACK IN
THE AMERICAN MIDWEST

Farmer Bill?

"I'm Coraline Corn.
The owner of Popcorn & Co.
We have a letter here from Holland.
Seems there's a problem.
I'm going there to fix it."

"And because it's all *your* fault, you have
to come with me.
Otherwise I'll make sure you never sell
another kernel again!
Well, what are you waiting for?
Pack your bags!"

HUNGRY FOR MORE
✩ POPCORN BOB? ✩

COMING SOON

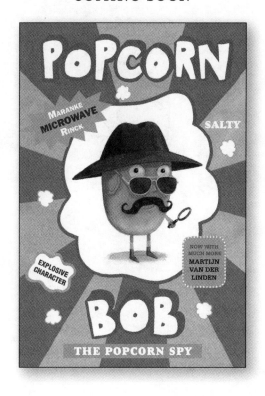